GREAT SCENES FROM
HORROR STORIES

John Green

Dover Publications
Garden City, New York

Note

Fans of horror and the supernatural will savor this chilling collection of some of the best scenes of the genre. Featuring exquisite black-and-white illustrations depicting 29 tales of terror by famed authors, this coloring book celebrates the creepy and the macabre. Some of the world's greatest horror writers—and their memorable stories—are represented here, including Mary Shelley's *Frankenstein,* Franz Kafka's *Metamorphosis,* and Bram Stoker's *Dracula.* Accompanied by a brief excerpt from the tale, the images have been arranged alphabetically by the author's name. So, prepare yourself for a spine-tingling journey into mystery and suspense, where dark drama lurks beneath the surface.

Bibliographical Note
Great Scenes from Horror Stories is a new work, first published by Dover Publications in 2012.

International Standard Book Number
ISBN-13: 978-0-486-48840-0
ISBN-10: 0-486-48840-3

Manufactured in the United States of America
48840306   2023
www.doverpublications.com

He opened his eyes in the darkness and saw above him a gleam of light, but how distant, how inaccessible!

Moxon sat facing me at the farther side of a small table upon which a single candle made all the light that was in the room. Opposite him, his back toward me, sat another person. On the table between the two was a chessboard.

Creeping with silent feet over the shifting sands, drawing imperceptibly nearer by soft, unhurried movements, the willows had come closer during the night. But had the wind moved them, or had they moved of themselves?

THE WILLOWS by Algernon Blackwood

"I am hungry," she murmured, "oh, so hungry; but now, Paul Sergevitch, your heart is mine."

"Your hour is upon you! Ye shall be mowed down like ripe corn, and the shadow of your name shall be swept from the earth! The glass of your iniquity is turned, and when its sand is run through, not a man of ye shall be!"

Day after day, day after day,
We stuck, nor breath nor motion;
As idle as a painted ship
Upon a painted ocean.
Water, water, every where,
And all the boards did shrink;
Water, water, every where,
Nor any drop to drink.

THE RIME OF THE ANCIENT MARINER by Samuel Taylor Coleridge   7

In the month of December in the year 1873, the British ship Dei Gratia steered into Gibraltar, having in tow the derelict brigantine [ship] Marie Celeste.

J. HABAKUK JEPHSON'S STATEMENT by Sir Arthur Conan Doyle

"I was as powerless as a child, and if, at any moment, a thought of turning back shot through my brain, one sight of that twitching face cast back upon its shoulder was sufficient to make me follow as though I were drawn along by some great mesmeric force."

THE WOMAN WITH A CANDLE by W. Bourne Cooke   9

It was Nina's doll-voice that had spoken. He would have known it among the voices of a hundred other dolls, yet there was something more in it, a little human ring with a pitiful cry, a call for help, and the wail of a hurt child.

THE DOLL'S GHOST by F. Marion Crawford

"Halloa! Below there! Look out! Look out!
For God's sake, clear the way!"

With quite startling suddenness, and as if she had risen from the earth, a woman stood before us, and demanded to know what we wanted there. She was the wildest, weirdest, strangest looking woman I have ever set eyes upon.

THE MYSTIC SPELL by Dick Donovan

He brandished the sword with a sort of cold fury and calculation; . . . reasoning that the source of the strange shadow must be between the table on which the lamp stood and the wall; . . . the blade gave out flashes of light, but the shadow remained unmoved.

"Are you mad, old man?" demanded Sir Edmund Andros. "How dare you stay the march of King James's Governor?" "I am here," said the old man, "because the cry of an oppressed people hath disturbed me in my secret place."

THE GRAY CHAMPION by Nathaniel Hawthorne

"I felt the cold, queer wind begin to blow upon me. To my astonishment, it seemed now to come from behind me, and I whipped 'round with a hideous quake of fear."

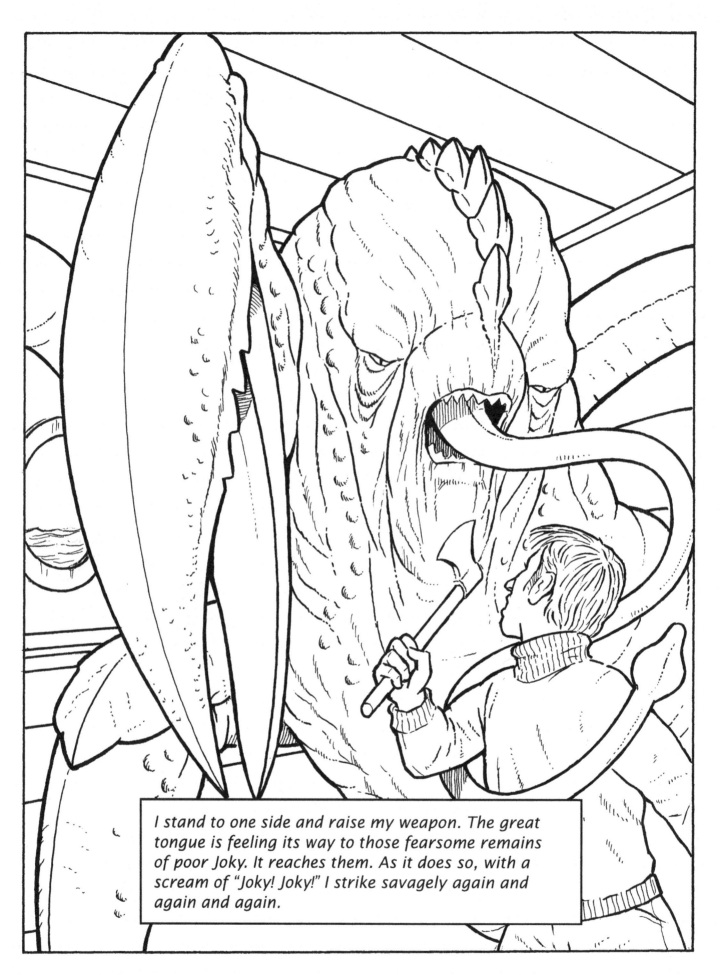

I stand to one side and raise my weapon. The great tongue is feeling its way to those fearsome remains of poor Joky. It reaches them. As it does so, with a scream of "Joky! Joky!" I strike savagely again and again and again.

On mounting a rising ground, which brought the figure of his fellow traveller in relief against the sky, gigantic in height, and muffled in a cloak, Ichabod was horror-struck on perceiving that he was headless!

No matter how hard he threw himself onto his right side, he always rolled onto his back again. He must have tried it a hundred times, closing his eyes so that he would not have to see the wriggling legs, and gave up only when he began to feel a light, dull pain in his side which he had never felt before.

"Take your friend away. He has done with Hanuman, but Hanuman has not done with him!"

THE CALL OF CTHULHU by H. P. Lovecraft

The thing of the idols, the green, sticky spawn of the stars, had awaked to claim his own. The stars were right again, and what an age-old cult had failed to do by design, a band of innocent sailors had done by accident. After vigintillions of years, great Cthulhu was loose again, and ravening for delight.

For a moment I was paralyzed. But the next instant I had recovered my presence of mind. I believed that Arthur and Tom had been playing some of their tricks upon me. They had burnt a red light outside my window, and were roaring with laughter.

Arising from the bed, tottering, with feeble steps, with closed eyes, and with the manner of one bewildered in a dream, the thing that was enshrouded advanced boldly and palpably into the middle of the apartment.

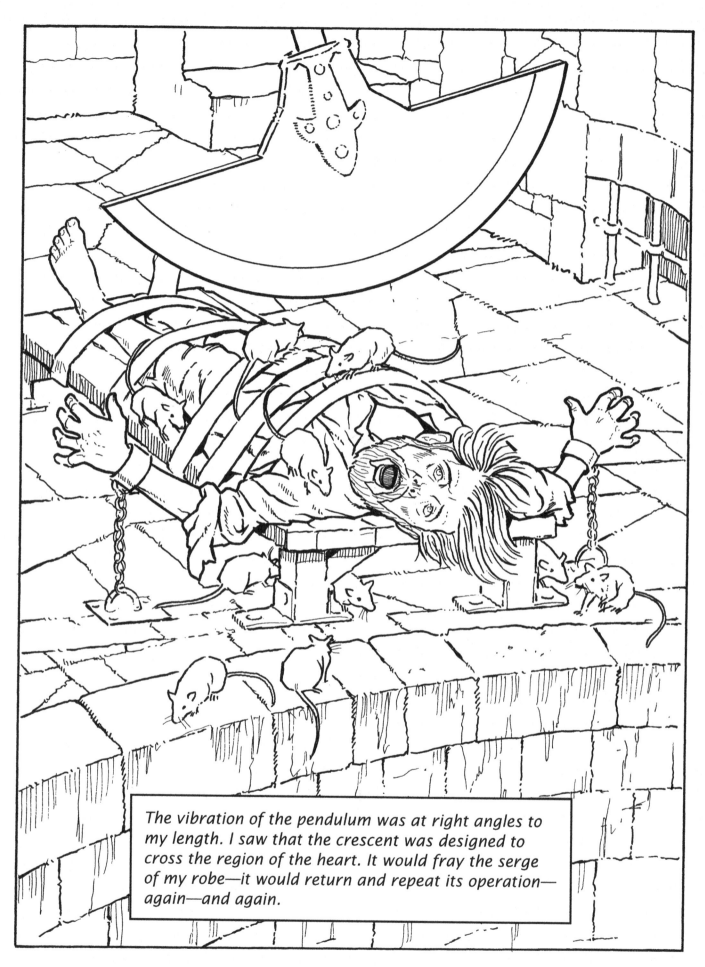

The vibration of the pendulum was at right angles to my length. I saw that the crescent was designed to cross the region of the heart. It would fray the serge of my robe—it would return and repeat its operation—again—and again.

And the Raven, never flitting, still is sitting, still is sitting
On the pallid bust of Pallas just above my chamber door;
And his eyes have all the seeming of a demon's that is dreaming,
And the lamplight o'er him streaming throws his shadow on the floor;
And my soul from out that shadow that lies floating on the floor
Shall be lifted—nevermore!

THE RAVEN by Edgar Allan Poe   25

"No one dared stop them, for they were corpses walking in the sunlight."

"As she approached I obtained a clearer view of her, but the nearer she came the more beautiful she seemed. It was the type of face for love of which men commit crimes; the dangerous beauty of a Circe; the witching countenance of a Siren."

"It was on a dreary night of November that I beheld the accomplishment of my toils, . . . my candle was nearly burnt out, when, by the glimmer of the half-extinguished light, I saw the dull yellow eye of the creature open; it breathed hard, and a convulsive motion agitated its limbs."

I lingered but a moment at the mirror: the second and conclusive experiment had yet to be attempted; it yet remained to be seen if I had lost my identity beyond redemption.

As we burst into the room, the Count turned his face, and the hellish look that I had heard described seemed to leap into it. His eyes flamed red with devilish passion.

DRACULA by Bram Stoker

The gloom which surrounded that horrible charnel pit, which seemed to go down to the very bowels of the earth, conveyed from far down the sights and sounds of the nethermost hell.

Many of the stories depicted in this coloring book are available in Dover editions. For further reading, please see the bibliography below.

Go to **www.doverpublications.com** for more information.

PAGES 2 AND 3:
   Ghost and Horror Stories of Ambrose Bierce, Ambrose Bierce [0-486-20767-6]

PAGES 4 AND 19:
   Great Horror Stories: Tales by Stoker, Poe, Lovecraft and Others, Edited by John Grafton [0-486-46143-2]

PAGES 6, 9, 12, 16, 22, AND 27:
   Gaslit Horror: Stories by Robert W. Chambers, Lafcadio Hearn, Bernard Capes and Others, Edited by Hugh Lamb [0-486-46305-2]

PAGE 7:
   The Rime of the Ancient Mariner, Samuel Taylor Coleridge [0-486-27266-4]

PAGE 8:
   The Best Supernatural Tales of Arthur Conan Doyle, Sir Arthur Conan Doyle [0-486-23725-7]

PAGE 11:
   Classic Ghost Stories by Wilkie Collins, M. R. James, Charles Dickens and Others, Edited by John Grafton [0-486-40430-7]

PAGES 13 AND 14:
   Great American Ghost Stories: Chilling Tales by Poe, Bierce, Hawthorne and Others, Edited by Mike Ashley [0-486-46602-7]

PAGE 17:
   The Legend of Sleepy Hollow and Other Stories, Washington Irving [0-486-46658-2]

PAGE 18:
   The Metamorphosis and Other Stories, Franz Kafka [0-486-29030-1]

PAGES 23 AND 24:
   The Gold-Bug and Other Tales, Edgar Allan Poe [0-486-26875-6]

PAGE 25:
   The Raven and Other Favorite Poems, Edgar Allan Poe [0-486-26685-0]

PAGE 28:
   Frankenstein, Mary Shelley [0-486-28211-2]

PAGE 29:
   The Strange Case of Dr. Jekyll and Mr. Hyde, Robert Louis Stevenson [0-486-26688-5]

PAGE 30:
   Dracula, Bram Stoker [0-486-41109-5]